DATE DUE

MAR 2 7 2008		
MAY 2 0 2008	FEB 2 7 2009	
APR 1 7 2008	NOV 4 2010	
	DEC 1 3 2010	
JUN 5 2008		
JUN 5 2008	SEP 2 9 2011	
OCT 1 5 2008	OCT 1 3 2011	
NOV 3 2008		
	OCT 2 0 2011	
JAN 2 8 2009	OCT 2 6 2011	
FEB 9 2010	JAN 1 1 2012	
OCT 0 6 2010	JAN 2 7 2012	
OCT 0 7 2010		
NOV 2 2010	OCT 1 7 2013	
JAN 6 2014	NOV 4 2013	
DEC 0 3 2014	NOV 2 2 2013	

REX JONES
SOCCER SHOWDOWN

by Jonny Zucker

illustrated by Enzo Troiano
Cover illustration by Marcus Smith

Librarian Reviewer
Marci Peschke
Librarian, Dallas Independent School District
MA Education Reading Specialist, Stephen F. Austin State University
Learning Resources Endorsement, Texas Women's University

Reading Consultant
Mary Evenson
Middle School Teacher, Edina Public Schools, MN
MA in Education, University of Minnesota

▼▼ STONE ARCH BOOKS
Minneapolis San Diego

First published in the United States in 2007
by Stone Arch Books,
151 Good Counsel Drive, P.O. Box 669,
Mankato, Minnesota 56002.
www.stonearchbooks.com

Originally published in Great Britain in 2005
by Badger Publishing Ltd.

Library of Congress Cataloging-in-Publication Data
Zucker, Jonny.
    [Football Frenzy]
    Soccer Showdown / by Jonny Zucker; illustrated by Enzo Troiano.
    p. cm. — (Keystone Books (Rex Jones))
    Originally published: Great Britain: Badger Publishing Ltd., 2005,
under the title Football Frenzy.
    Summary: Fifteen-year-old Rex Jones and his friends Dave and Carl
are transported by Rex's mysterious cell phone onto a soccer team that is
headed for the championships—if they can avoid being killed by a bully
on the opposing team.
    ISBN-13: 978-1-59889-334-2 (library binding)
    ISBN-10: 1-59889-334-3 (library binding)
    ISBN-13: 978-1-59889-430-1 (paperback)
    ISBN-10: 1-59889-430-7 (paperback)
    [1. Adventure and adventurers Fiction. 2. Soccer—Fiction.
3. Sportsmanship—Fiction. 4. Cellular telephones—Fiction.] I. Troiano,
Enzo, ill. II. Title.
PZ7.Z77925Soc 2007
[Fic]—dc22
                                    2006026736

1 2 3 4 5 6 12 11 10 09 08 07

Printed in the United States of America

TABLE OF CONTENTS

How It All Began

Fifteen-year-old Rex Jones used to have a pretty normal life. He went to school. He hung out with his best friends, Carl and Dave. He played sports. He watched TV. Normal stuff.

Then, a few months ago, Rex bought a new cell phone. It was the last one the store had. Rex had seen the phone in a magazine, but his new phone was different in one way.

It had two extra buttons. One said EXPLORE and one said RETURN. The man in the store said that none of the other phones had those buttons.

The phone worked fine at first. Rex forgot about the extra buttons.

One day the phone started to make a strange buzzing sound. When Rex looked at it, the green EXPLORE button was flashing.

He pressed it, and suddenly found himself in an incredible dream world of adventures. Each adventure could only be ended when Rex's phone buzzed again and the flashing red RETURN button was pressed.

He never knows when an adventure will begin, and he never knows if it will end in time to save him.

CHAPTER 1

In the Tunnel

Rex, Carl, and Dave sat on a bench in the locker room. It was halftime of the soccer match. Their school was losing one to nothing.

"You were awful," their coach, Mr. Hill, shouted at the team. "In the second half, you need to work much, much harder."

Suddenly, the green EXPLORE button on Rex's cell phone lit up.

He felt it buzz and pulled it out of his jacket.

"Go for it," said Carl. Rex pressed the button.

There was a flash of white light and the next thing they knew, the boys found themselves in the tunnel of a huge stadium with other soccer players.

Rex, Carl, and Dave and the rest of their team were in blue uniforms of Central. The other team was wearing white uniforms that said United.

"It's the last game of the season," whispered Rex.

"And we're playing for Central!" said Carl.

"This is the biggest game of the year," said Dave.

"Yeah," said Rex, nodding.

"If Central wins they stay first in the league," said Dave.

"But if Central loses or ties," said Rex, "they go down."

Rex was about to say something else when a harsh voice called his name.

CHAPTER 2

Parker Problem

United's captain, Steve Parker, walked over to Rex.

Rex had never liked the way Steve played. He was always getting into trouble and yelling at the referees.

"I hear you're playing on the right today," Steve said.

"Am I?" asked Rex.

"Stop trying to be funny," said Steve.

Rex wanted to say he really didn't know where he was playing, but Steve was in his face again.

"Don't even think about playing well," whispered Steve.

"Or what?" asked Rex.

"Or you won't have any legs after the game," Steve growled.

Rex stared at Steve. "You don't scare me," he said. "The best team will win."

"I don't think so," said Steve, moving closer to Rex. "You're going to lose this game and Central will never make the championships."

CHAPTER 3

Kick Off

The referee called the two teams and they began to walk out of the tunnel and out into the stadium. They were greeted by the incredible sound of sixty thousand cheering fans.

Photographers clicked their cameras wildly, following every move the players made.

"Can I have the two captains, please," called the referee.

"Go up there, Rex," a couple of Central players called.

Rex walked to the center circle. Steve Parker was already there. Steve scowled at Rex.

"Shake hands, men," said the ref. Rex held out his hand. Steve looked at it as if it was poison. He shook Rex's hand quickly.

"Heads or tails, Steve?" asked the ref, pulling out a coin.

"Tails," said Steve.

The ref tossed the coin in the air. It was tails.

Steve smiled. "We'll kick off," he told the ref.

Halftime Havoc

The game moved quickly. The players were excited, and the tackles were fast. Five minutes before halftime, the ball flew into the United penalty area. Steve Parker tried to trip Carl, but Carl flew forward and bumped the ball with his head.

The ball crashed into the back of the United net. The Central players yelled with joy and piled onto Carl.

The Central fans went crazy.

"Great goal!" yelled Rex, slapping Carl on the back.

A minute later, Rex picked up the ball on the right and started running toward the corner flag.

Out of nowhere, Rex heard footsteps thundering toward him, and Steve Parker pushed him to the ground. The ref didn't see it.

Rex's right ankle hurt. He thought he twisted it.

"Sorry, Jones," Steve said. He didn't sound sorry. "Accidents happen."

Rex stood up. He wasn't going to let Parker bother him.

Then, just before halftime, the Central goalie, Mick, jumped up to grab the ball from a United player.

But the ball slipped through his fingers. The ball wobbled to a United forward, who tapped it into the goal.

It was a terrible goal to give away.

As Mick picked the ball up out of the back of the net, the ref blew his whistle. It was halftime.

The Central players headed for the locker room. Kevin Talbot, the Central manager, screamed at Mick.

"Leave him alone!" said Rex. "We all make mistakes."

"Keep your nose out of this, Jones," growled Talbot. "You may be the team captain, but I'm the manager."

"It was a mistake," Rex replied. "We all make mistakes."

Talbot looked at Rex in amazement. No one had ever spoken to him like that before.

CHAPTER 5

Rex's Goal

With less than fifteen minutes to go, Central and United were tied.

Carl passed the ball to Rex.

Rex ran past two United players. He went around a third. The crowd was screaming.

Then Rex saw Steve Parker out of the corner of his eye.

Steve was running toward him.

Rex could tell that if Steve got him, Rex would be hurt. Badly. So Rex jumped in the air as high as he could.

Steve's body slid under Rex's body.

Steve went flying into the ground. His body hit it with a thwack. Steve yelled out in pain.

"Oh sorry, Parker," Rex called out, "accidents happen."

The ref ran over as Steve got to his feet and held up a yellow card.

"What's that for?" shouted Steve.

"I've had my eye on you all afternoon," said the ref. "You're a dirty player, Parker, and a cheat."

"Send Parker home!" yelled the Central fans.

Steve looked up at them and spat on the ground.

Dave kicked the ball. It sped along the field and reached Carl. He ran past a United player and passed the ball over to Rex.

Rex was thirty yards away from the goal.

He looked up and saw the United goalie standing in front of his net.

Rex shot.

The ball hurtled through the air.

For a second it seemed like it was going to miss, but it curved back and squeezed between the United goalie and the post.

It was an amazing goal.

The Central fans yelled with delight.

CHAPTER 6

The Last Seconds

Rex looked up at the giant clock in the stadium. There was only one minute to go.

"Come on, guys," yelled Rex. "One more minute and we're safe."

But a United player kicked the ball into the penalty area.

Mick Ronson jumped up and punched it away, but as he did, he fell to the ground.

The ball spun in the air and landed at Steve Parker's feet.

Mick was still on the ground.

Steve Parker pulled his foot back to kick the ball.

Rex knew he had to act fast. He heard the thud of Steve's foot making contact with the ball.

Rex jumped forward. The blur of the ball raced toward him as he flew through the air.

The ball smashed into his left foot and sailed toward the goal. Instead of getting farther away from Mick, the ball was headed straight for him.

"No!" cried Rex. He closed his eyes.

They had tied, and Central wouldn't be first.

He'd ruined it for Central.

CHAPTER 7

Red Card

Rex lay on the ground, his face in the mud. He felt terrible.

Suddenly he felt a pat on his back. Then another. And another. He heard Carl and Dave and the rest of the Central players shouting and laughing.

He opened his eyes. The ball was behind the goal. His foot had directed Parker's shot over the bar.

It was still 2-1, and Central was winning. Rex got to his feet.

Steve Parker looked furious. All of the United players were shouting at him. "You missed an open goal, Parker!" one of them yelled. "We won't forget this!"

Parker grabbed the ball and kicked it high into the crowd.

The ref quickly reached into his pocket and showed Parker the red card.

"You're lucky you lasted this long," snapped the ref. "This means you'll miss the first three games of next season."

Steve scowled at the ref and walked off the field in disgust.

CHAPTER 8

Central Saved

A new ball was thrown onto the field from behind Mick's goal. Mick stood up and limped over to it.

"I'll take the goal kick," shouted Rex.

"Get on with it!" shouted the referee. "There's thirty seconds left!"

Forget thirty seconds, thought Rex as he kicked the ball into the air. He felt like he could play for thirty years!

As the ref blew his whistle for the end of the game, Rex and the Central players ran over to their fans. The fans were dancing and singing. And they were chanting Rex's name.

Rex had saved the game for Central.

Kevin Talbot came over and shook Rex's hand. "You were amazing out there," Talbot said, smiling.

As soon as Rex and the Central team got back into the locker room, Rex saw the red RETURN button flashing on his cell phone.

He pressed it.

There was a flash of white light and the boys found themselves back on the field at school.

"Don't be too much of a hot shot, Rex," shouted Mr. Hill, as Rex ran past another player and kicked the ball past the opposing goalie and into the goal.

"What, do you think you're playing for United?" called Mr. Hill.

"No, Mr. Hill," Rex called back. "I think I'll stick with Central!"

About the Author

Even as a child, Jonny Zucker wanted to be a writer. Today, he has written more than 30 books. He has also spent time working as a teacher, song writer, and stand-up comedian. Jonny lives in London with his wife and two children.

About Marcus Smith

Marcus Smith says that he started drawing when his mother put a pen in his hand when he was a baby. Smith grew up in Chicago, where he took classes at the world famous Art Institute. In Chicago he also designed band logos and tattoos! He moved west and studied at the Minneapolis College of Art and Design, majoring in both Illustration and Comic Art. As an artist, Smith was "influenced by the land of superheroes, fantasy, horror, and action," and he continues to work in the world of comics.

Glossary

captain (KAP-tuhn)—the leader of a sports team

fate (FAYT)—what will happen to a person

goalie (GOH-lee)—someone who guards the goal to keep the other team from scoring

havoc (HAV-uk)—confusion; things wildly out of control

manager (MAN-uh-jur)—the person who is in charge of a team's training and performance

opposing (uh-POZE-ing)—in soccer, the other team

penalty (PEN-uhl-tee)—a punishment a team or player suffers for breaking the rules

referee (ref-uh-REE)—someone who makes sure that a game is played by the rules

yellow cards and **red cards** are given as punishments when a player breaks the rules. A yellow card is a warning, and a red card means the player must leave the game.

Discussion Questions

1. Why was it so important for Central to win the game?

2. What do you think about Steve Parker's behavior during the game? What should he have done differently?

3. If the game had ended differently, and Central had lost, how do you think Rex would have felt?

Writing Prompts

1. What's your favorite sports team? Write a story in which, like Rex, you suddenly become a member of your favorite team during a very important game. What position would you play? Describe what you would be wearing and what the location would be. How would you make sure that your team won the game?

2. Rex's cell phone sometimes gets him in trouble, but sometimes, like in this story, it brings him to amazing events. Where would you go, if you had a magical cell phone just like Rex's?

Also by
Jonny Zucker

Skatebard Power

Nick Jones was all set to win the skateboard competition, until the bully, Dan Abbot, stepped in and ruined his chances. And his board. With no board, Nick has no hope. Time is running out!

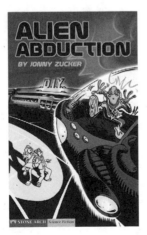

Alien Abduction

When Shelly and Dan are abducted by Zot the alien, they teach him about the ways of earthling teenagers. Hopefully they can convince Mr. Tann of their story before they end up in big trouble!

More Rex Jones Adventures

Spin Off

Rex's incredible cell phone transports him to the backstage of an awesome club, where he'll be showing off his DJ skills in front of a live audience. Rex is thrilled, until he realizes that one of his opponents wants to win, whatever the cost.

Safecrackers

Rex Jones's cell phone sends him and his friends to the high-powered security center of a bank. The three boys are in charge of making sure that Razor Bell, a bank robber who's a master of disguise, can't steal the bank's hundred million dollars!

Internet Sites

Do you want to know more about subjects related to this book? Or are you interested in learning about other topics? Then check out FactHound, a fun, easy way to find Internet sites.

Our investigative staff has already sniffed out great sites for you!

Here's how to use FactHound:

1. Visit *www.facthound.com*

2. Select your grade level.

3. To learn more about subjects related to this book, type in the book's ISBN number: **1598893343**.

4. Click the **Fetch It** button.

FactHound will fetch the best Internet sites for you!